Los Elementos
By Grace Marsh

Quiero Vivir

I want to live,
to break free, to
soar high,
high above the clouds.

I want to feel the rain
beating down
like a drum upon my enervated flesh,
to blush like a rose in winter
as snowflakes kiss its
shivering frame.

I want to discover a waterfall,
all rushing stream and hidden rock -
I want to fall in love with
a Spanish flame and
allow it to scorch
my waning gaze,
my waxing breath,
with its hungry,
hungry tongue.

I want to be selfish,
to hold myself
when nobody else will,
to dance alone
as dusk falls and my arms are empty;
I want to be human before being
half,
to be significant without needing an other.

I want to love the world around *and* inside of me.
I want to live -
God, I want to live.

El Aire

No Sobre el Amor

Ella es la brisa,
la brisa dulce, dulce -
ella es el aire,
el aire puro, puro:
ella puede calmarme, salvarme;
ella es la brisa,
la brisa en mi pelo.

Rápido, nítido,
bonito, tranquilo,
ella es el aire.

Not About Love (Translation)

She is the breeze,
the sweet, sweet breeze -
she is the air,
the pure, pure air:
she can calm me, save me;
she is the breeze,
the breeze in my hair.

Short, sharp,
beautiful, tranquil,
she is the air.

Carpool

We are crammed in,
side by side,
voices blending into one another
as we shout to be heard
over the music.

He starts to sing along,
then her,
now, me -
suddenly,
all of us are screaming as
loudly as we can,
and the sound is
speeding past the
road,
over the
trees,
away from the houses and
bewildered dogs and
ogling schoolchildren with their
disapproving mothers.

The windows are down,
air is
rushing into our lungs -
filling us up,
pulling us towards the sky.

I am weightless,
unlimited,
balloon-like in my haste -
I am gliding,
soaring like our voices:
she is holding my hand and
laughing;
his feet are slung lazily across the dashboard.
She drives,
he directs,
she traces a pattern with her thumb,
he changes the song,
I tell them all,
every last one,
just how light we are.
They understand.

We all breathe.

Sisters

Daughters of oxygen,
of gale and of breeze -
three enervated
dandelion seeds winnowing in the wind.

I blow thrice, one wish for each of you:
for the first,
love;
for the second,
catharsis;
for the third,
recognition;
I wear all three of you
pressed into a pendant
around my neck,
enclosed in a spherical glass house,
where the sky is the granter of all wishes, and
dandelion seeds float freely in its
midst.

Day and Night

For Lindley

When starless skies
smother me in black,
in ink, in absence,
I search for
your dawn,
your break,
your simple, healing ray:
I find it
in secrets; in laughter;
in the clasp of a hand or
in the squeal of delight:
I find it in everything you
do, are and embody;
I find *it* and
it is joy, bliss, catharsis.

Eighty times
the sun rises,
eighty times
darkness fades,
eighty times
I sit down and
eighty times
you smile big, smile happy,
smile sunshine.

Dreamcatcher

Her lids flutter closed,
body resting heavy on her mattress -
enervated, irresponsible.

You press your lips to her jawline,
softening every harsh edge with your breath.
You dance from one
temple to another,
little, light steps,
fairy-like,
so as not to wake her.

Her hair falls across the pillow,
tangled and welcoming,
lifted slightly by your hands:
you brush your fingers through it.

She stirs,
sighs,
rests again.

Dawn nears, and
her freckles glow with its
backlight -
luminescent.
Never before have you seen
sunshine
look so
human.

You turn on your heel,
fly away.

Her lids struggle open -
eyes instantly seeking the window.
She sees you there,
suspended,
your very essence caught up in a
maze of string and feathers.

She smiles,
sits up,
spends the day
describing the
silent sylph of her dream.

By the time she returns,
you have bribed the breeze into
sweeping you away.

Starlight

I have never seen the stars.
Or, if I have, I don't remember.
But sometimes,
at night,
I'll close my eyes and
delight in the
sight of
constellations.

In them, I see you:
first, a young girl, features
dimpled and creased with happiness,
smiling,
running towards your big sister with arms outstretched,
ready to carry the burden of her day on your
slender shoulders.

Second, an only-just woman,
same grin, same run, same embrace,
only this time,
you greet your man with a kiss -
I call him your man because you
wore the trousers, you made the rules,
you, strong, invincible one,
you,
you who healed every hurt.

You, shooting star,
you, holder of hands and children and faces,
you, wiper of tears, lover of sisters, boss of lovers,
you.

I see you, comet, supernova,
Lily,
flying across the sealed expanse of my of my eyelids and
I know, I will always know,
that I have seen the stars,
and that I remember them, too.

Rainbow

I see you,
Red.
I see you fighting,
lips pressed together
in determination,
eyes overbrimming with
Pride -
I see you, the Orange warrior,
whose words
echo through the streets,
whose Song silences the
oppressors,
I see you,
incandescent one,
Yellow and bright.

I see Green people
who Love
unabashedly,
dance freely,
speak
so truly -
I see Blue kisses on
Indigo cheeks,
and I see
you,
Violet.
I see you,
Strong,
I see you,
Brave…

I see you,
Colour.

Blown Away

My feet are lifted
from the ground -
I am airborne,
invincible.

I am the wind
whipping through your hair,
the gale
screaming in your ear -
I am all tornado,
all woman,
and
I will be seen.
I will be heard.
I will be felt.

Lungs: On Breathing In

Steady now,
my love -
inhale
slowly, softly,
and try not to be scared
as you do.

The rattling of your ribcage is
merely a lullaby,
my love,
the rasping of your throat
just a hymn.

Be careful,
careful now,
my love -
calm down, take a breath,
I'm here.

I'm holding on to your hand now,
my love,
and I promise to never let go.
Just keep composing
for me -
that's right, that's it -
keep breathing,
my love,
keep breathing,
for you,
well,
you are infinite.

Lady Jane

Dear Wind,
raise me up,
take me away -
lead me to the world that is
invisible:
I want to be sure of bliss,
I want to dwell in paradise;
Dear Wind,
lead me to paradise,
Dear Wind,
show the sky my prayer,
Dear Wind,
raise me up.

When my soul takes flight,
raise me up,
when I honour my God,
raise me up,
when the axe comes down,
raise me up -
Dear Wind,
give me my sanctuary,
Dear Wind,
show me the way to
Heaven.

El Agua

Espacio Seguro

Me quedo aquí,
mejilla a mejilla con las olas.
Este no es un lugar para ser
temido:
no hay peligro aquí.
Peligro aquí
es una palabra extranjera;
peligro aquí
no encaja bien en nuestras bocas,
no tiene sabor nativo en nuestras lenguas;
peligro aquí
no existe en todo.

Aquí,
todo lo que existe son
las olas, las mejillas -
mis mejillas y las suyas -
y las canciones,
canciones del agua, del amor, del Dios.

Todos los días,
sono aquellas canciones,
canto aquellas canciones,
y - cuando he terminado con una boca seca, una lengua sed -
bebo el agua,
el agua con la sal,
el agua con el aire,
el agua con la libertad y la esperanza -
bebo y gusto la esperanza;
me encanta el gusto de la esperanza,
del agua, del amor, del Dios...

Todos los días,
nado.
Nado y respiro
debajo del mar -
yo soy una chica *y* un pez
al mismo tiempo:
yo soy una sirena, tal vez.

Aquí,
puedo ser una sirena si quiero,
aquí,
no sé el significado del peligro,
o pérdida, o pena, o dolor.
Sólo sé que yo soy
una sirena, tal vez,
nadando mejilla a mejilla con las olas,
cantando sus canciones
sin peligro,

sin miedo,
sin ayuda.

Safe Space (Translation)

I stay here,
cheek to cheek with the waves.
This isn't a place to be
scared of:
there is no danger here.
Danger here
is a foreign word;
danger here
doesn't fit right in our mouths,
doesn't taste right on our tongues;
danger here
doesn't exist at all.

Here,
all that exists are
the waves, the cheeks -
my cheeks and theirs -
and songs,
songs of water, of love, of God.

Every day,
I hear those songs,
I sing those songs,
and - when I have finished with a dry mouth, a thirsty tongue -
I drink the water,
the water with salt,
the water with air,
the water with freedom and hope -
I drink and I taste hope;
I love the taste of hope,
of water, of love, of God.

Every day,
I swim.
I swim and I breathe
beneath the sea -
I am a girl *and* a fish
at the same time:
I am a mermaid, perhaps.

Here,
I can be a mermaid if I want,
here,
I don't know the meaning of danger,
or loss, or shame, or pain.
I only know that I am
a mermaid, perhaps,

swimming cheek to cheek with the waves,
singing their songs,
without danger,
without fear,
without help.

The First Cup

The somnolent pushing of a button,
the distracted froth and gargle,
boiling water poured into a mug and
spiced with oriental flower
or softened by blackberry and vanilla.

The morning is early, new,
the day incomplete and unchartered;
your house is sleepy,
silent save a
practised purr or padding paw -
you finish seven eighths' worth of the drink,
an old, unbreakable habit,
leave the cup on the table and
close the door behind you.

Synaesthesia

They say your eyes are
blue, azure, Pacific in their depth -
I will never see your sea-foam orbs,
I will never meet your Atlantic gaze,
I will never need to.

Your voice speaks
in tide, in ebb, in break, in roll and fall,
my friend,
you are a child of the water:
the Southern's poetic licence,
the daughter of Indian horizon and whale song.

My friend,
my friend I have never
craved to look at you -
you are the only one
with inflection enough to rival tsunamis,
my friend -
I thank you for your
constant, resonating presence;
I am estranged from the beach but
not your waving, rising melody.
My friend,
your melody pervades darkness,
silence,
my friend,
your eyes are blue, azure, oceanic in their depth
but your soul is loud, auditory, and
comforting in its song.

August

Ice -
a glacial glass clouded with cold,
condensation kissing fledgling fingertips,
the holding of heady hands to hot cheeks.

The summer sings in aquamarine eyes
and its light liquifies
until undine undulations
weave waves in the water:
you part your lips and swallow.

Mermaid

Her hair falls across
my tongue in vague, accidental tangles, and so I
tuck it gently behind the
spirals of her seashell ear
(the left one, as always).
With every kiss I taste the ocean,
with every breath I feel the tide:
if this is blindness then let it be so;
I am no longer afraid of darkness
or of diving into oceanic depths -
I am no longer afraid to be vulnerable,
and I know that
she feels the same.

I know this because her
every unsaid word
stutters in the space between us;
I know this because the
weak spots on my neck are
tattooed with her name,
and I know this because her sea salt hand is my safe refuge,
my lighthouse, my shelter from the storm.

We Sell Seashells

We lie on our backs,
faces upturned towards the sky as if in
prayer;
you press your hot little ear to mine,
and I swear that I can hear the
ocean leaping, tripping,
stumbling
in the heady space just between our skulls.

For Eleanor

I give you
tempests, hurricanes, unrivalled storms:
rain lashing, waves raging.

You are graceful in your conduct,
able
- with calm breath and measured speech -
to quell the ocean's fury,
to tranquillise the sky's sobs;
you give me
lakes, rivers, gently ebbing streams,
you give me
sense, order -
you give me reason.

When I am the
tempest, the hurricane, the unrivalled storm,
you talk me down,
placid, accidentally amusing,
tell me to forget the rain, the waves,
ask me to focus on the
here, the now, the tangible,
remind me that there's a time for swimming,
and that this isn't it.

I learn from you:
I learn to give you
Shakespeare, plot twists, self-penned poetry -
no water, no storm.

The Deluge

You'll remember me when it rains, my darling,
you'll remember me with the spattered windows,
with the jumping droplets, the waltzing water,
the lashing liquid beating down upon your bowed head,
you'll remember me when it rains and
the thought will make you
shine.

My rays will cast rainbows across the glassy panes,
and grey will suddenly be more multifarious than the spectra -
your dull orbs will glimmer softly in the harsh sunlight,
your head will be thrown back, flailing limbs akimbo as you spin,
your tongue catching rainwater as if each bead were a diamond,
and your feet splashing fruitlessly across the saturated ground.

I will have fallen from grace, from the clouds,
I will have rocketed straight downwards, spiralling head-first and
helpless;
I will land so heavily that china cups
can be made from my splintering bones,
and saucers can be fashioned from my misshapen skull.

You have always loved
skeletons, and imperfections, and rain.
I have always loved hiding, and falling, and pouring out
my *everything*.

So, you'll remember me when it rains, my darling,
you'll remember me, and you'll fall out of love with the petrichor
as it reminds you that
I'm gone.

Evaporate, Condense

I try to leave.
I try to leave
time and time
again -
I disappear,
gaseous, insipid,
but your warmth
always seems to
pull me back, to
press me
against a window, or
along the inside of a mug.

I try to leave,
I fail -
you wipe me away,
wash me up,
but still,
running, steaming, hoping,
I return.

I, Virginia

Dearest,

I feel certain now -
I am no longer afraid.
The water here is cool, crystalline;
I close my eyes and
feel it kissing their lids,
caressing my arms,
embracing my torso -
oh darling,
if anything could
save me
it would be this:
this drifting, this river, this chill.
I am no longer afraid,
truly, I am not.
My lungs fill, swell, disgorge their air,
but I am not afraid -
I am tired, waning, ready,
but not afraid,
never afraid.

V

La Tierra

El Suelo

Tiendes aquí,
sin juicio,
debajo de mis pies -
te quedas aquí,
sin juicio,
debajo de mis pies,
y puedo oírte reír
como mis pasos
te traen a la vida:
tocándote;
mostrándote...
mostrándote el camino.

Nunca dejaré de
mostrarte el camino.

The Ground (Translation)

You lay here,
without judgement,
beneath my feet -
you stay here,
without judgement,
beneath my feet,
and I can hear you laugh
as my steps bring you to life:
touching you;
showing you…
showing you the way.

I will never stop
showing you the way.

Apple Cider in Summertime

That summer,
we drank cheap apple cider and
laughed at the way it bubbled.
We lay with our
hands intertwined,
stretched out across the grass,
and you,
my damned dendrologist,
whispered with the leaves and
serenaded me with odes to the Oak,
fabrications of the Fur,
stories for the Sycamore -
I think I loved you then:
a tipsy, somnolent and hopeful
kind of love;
a heady, heavy kind of love.

That summer,
we picked fruit from branches
and revelled in its
sweetness -
you revelled in my
sweetness,
darling
I was sweet once,
too.

That summer,
the canker came,
the rot ate at my smooth flesh and
forced me to
mould
myself into the person you wanted me to be;
into the person who was worth more than just a summer.
The scourge chew and bit and ripped
but I still wasn't good enough for you,
and so I fell,
I fell like apples, rolled like conkers and died like leaves,
finally allowing the
disease to
usurp my happiness,
darling you
usurped my happiness.
You,
with your bitter alcohol and your empty promises cutting through
the cloying, crepuscular air;
you,
with your lamplight kisses and hungry lips;
you,
who needed Summer but yearned for Autumn,

you,
who never loved me -
not even for an instant,
not even tipsily, somnolently -
darling,
you didn't even love me
distractedly.

On Bad Days and Flora

I have joined the fallen ones:
the crushed daises and
uprooted tulips.
I have joined the broken ones:
the sapless barks and
crumbling soil -
each one of them marks another
fledgling love,
another vice on which to
hook myself.

I have joined the silent ones:
those who never speak but always think;
those who sit in flower beds just
waiting to be
trampled.

I have joined the muddy ones:
the murky streams and insidious bogs;
I have breathed in
quicksand and
lived to tell the tale;
I have kissed poison ivy and
enjoyed the way it
burned;
I have been here before, and
I will be here again,
turning my back on the sunflowers in favour of the
thorns,
joining the hapless and just
waiting to be saved.

Bloom, Whither

Today,
I think of you as
wisp, as
Angelou's rising dust, as
soil caught in fingernail -
tomorrow,
I will think of you as
grass, as
flower sprouting from the ground, as
leaf and stem and petal...

The day after tomorrow,
the sun will not
shine,
the rain will not
pour,
we will not
blossom
and I will not think of you as
anything.

The Chosen Ones

Here are the fields where
men with blackberry hands go
picking at nighttime.
They take daisies, usually,
tulips when they can.

Those poor,
pretty little flower girls
shrink as they see them near,
reverting to buds and
bowing their stems in
preemptive shame -
but the men,
the men with
stained fingertips and forceful grips,
are keen.
They plunge themselves into the ground:
tearing; ripping;
blind, perhaps;
deaf, surely;
everyone else can hear their
screams.

There aren't many daisies left now, and even
fewer tulips.
Yet
the men with blackberry hands
refuse to be moved -
they claim these fields as their
own, name the very ground after their fathers and grandfathers,
almost as though
they have the right to
wildflowers,
to soil and to fruit.
I shan't argue with them -
even bluebells are vulnerable
when they have
voices.

Consenescere

Consenescere - To grow old and grey together, to stay too long in an occupation, or to decay, lose respect, fade away.

Our Lily is a wraithlike flower, sleeping in the pale soil of a hospital bed,
waiting to bloom in the deathly silence.
Her roots are linked with palms and fingers,
her unmistakable scent hidden somewhere in the
quicksand that is her body,
and her leaves lying - black like a funeral, green like the life she cannot live -
beside her.

She is neither old enough nor grey enough for this:
her petals are still unfurling in the cold morning glow;
her parched stem is still writhing towards the light;
his lips are still hot against her forehead;
our love still sprawls coolly across her clammy skin.
She is not wrinkled or torn in the slightest -
her beauty remains untouchably fragile,
and we remember her former body
(a sum far greater than its parts)
as perfect as it was for as long as it was.

Enervated -
her epidermis exhausts every opportunity to flourish or photosynthesise,
it is able only to perspire and respire,
you see
Death is her new occupation,
and she has most definitely exasperated
all of its lunch breaks, reprises and reveries
in the eighty-nine days we've been here.
Her previous employers - Life, Love and Longing - didn't want to lose her.
But she still, somehow, ended up with Pain and Tumour and
all of the other pathogens that her parents warned her of.
She did *not* retire.
She was content with Life, with Love, with Longing.

Petals, leaves, roots, a stem,
they all seem to concave at once,
screaming, "Take me to Jesus, let me go to Jesus!"
His hot lips and our cool love don't register anymore,
the morphine - or is it ammonia? -
infects every one of her living cells
and causes her matter to become powder, or dust, or decay.

We cannot stop the detritivores from gnawing away -
she is fading so quickly -
but we water her out of respect,
out of love, out of anguish and distraction.

The photograph of our Lily sits in the place her vase used to be.

It is old and crumpled, wrinkled in the middle and torn at the edges,
so unlike her that it hurts.
The air smells like disinfectant - not flora - and the walls are hotter than his lips,
the floor cooler than our love.

We are falling apart, fading away in the breeze,
just as she did.

Sunflower

'I wish I could just be suspended in the feeling of you holding me forever.' - L

You are with me
every day -
your yellow petals
clothe me,
your green stem
is my shelter,
your soft centre, my bed:
I wear
fragments of you
in my hair,
taste pieces of you on my tongue;
I place you in a glass vase and
carry you in my arms.
My love, my sunflower,
I hold you
always.

Hospital Bed

Flowers are sent -
they bloom from the sheets,
a thousand floral reminders of
what
I
have
done.

I taste
chemicals and vomit,
feel my head splinter into
a million different pieces and
watch as the tulips whisper,
the orchids point,
the lilies weep -
I rip their heads from their bodies,
crush their leaves beneath my feet
and wish for
eternal reprieve.

Poppy Fields

The Earth is dry, sandy,
the Belgian air solemn and silent
in our lungs.
The way is guided, uneven,
full of dips and trees and barbed wire -
with each new step,
there are more
fallen soldiers who rise from the fields,
walk beside us and
recount their plights in
hollow tones.
Wilfred Owen speaks in meter,
his voice laden with
suppressed pain and sarcasm:
"Dulce et decorum est," he murmurs,
"Pro patria mori."

The poppies we are holding
fall from our hands,
landing -
bleeding and broken -
atop the soil.

Sappho's Garden

How lovely it feels
to picture her there,
unwrapping those fragile flower women
with her soothing words and lyre strings,
to see her watching as their petals
unfurl, blossom, fall upon her lap
in modest fell swoops.

How true it feels to imagine her then,
tending to lilacs and
somnolent poppies,
to look on as she
kisses them back to life.

How lovely,
how true,
how safe it feels
simply to think of her
at all.

El Fuego

Quemando

El calor se siente más dulce
como lo sostienes en tus manos:
morados, melocotones y corales;
todo lo sostienes en tus manos.

Las llamas más suaves que besitos
parpadean en tus ojos:
naranjas, amarillos y rojos;
todos parpadean en tus ojos.

El humo ve más bonito
cuando deja tus labios en nubes;
blancos, negros y grises;
todos dejan tus labios en nubes.

Burning (Translation)

The heat feels sweeter
as you hold it in your hands:
purples, peaches and corals;
you hold them all in your hands.

Flames sweeter than kisses
flicker in your eyes:
oranges, yellows and reds;
they all flicker in your eyes.

The smoke looks prettier
when it leaves your lips in clouds:
whites, blacks and greys;
they all leave your lips in clouds.

An Atheist's Mass

I don't sing along to the hymns,
or give my voice to the collective prayers
spoken in soft, solemn tones.
I cannot pretend to listen to the Bible recitals,
or the religious man's take on grief.
I refuse to assimilate myself with a
Faith I do not believe in,
but I will still light a candle for you,
Incandescent One.
I will still be the spark that starts the flame of your
memory,
I won't leave you to smoulder, to die out -
not this time.

This time,
things will be different.
This time, I can keep you
dancing, glowing, shining:
an infinite light, a forever fire.

So burn bright,
Angel,
burn long, burn hard, and
burn like the word 'flicker' never existed.

Ana

I will dive into you
headfirst and screaming:
lick my skin,
dissolve it;
burn my bones down to ashes,
your crematorium a
weighing scale,
your acrid stench that of
vomit in a toilet bowl.

Let me fall through your
flaming fingertips,
pyrolyse me
as I do -
entrap me,
engulf me,
ensconce me.

I need you to
ensconce me,
I need you to
become me,
I need
you
to take
control.

Ashes

Blistered feet tuck themselves beneath
barely-cool sheets,
caressing,
rubbing until their spark-shooting
heels
(kissed time and again by
white linen lips)
stop weeping and,
at last,
begin to
smile.

A head hits out steadily, staunchly,
a baseline thrumming across
temples and
around ears:
its song is that of
half-hearted regret and burning nausea;
a ceaseless, acidic beat
punching, piercing,
a perpetually pounding polyphony of
hangover and harsh light.

Voices clamour relentlessly, asking for
tea with milk,
toast with jam -
its crumbs pyrolyse their
raw throats,
scorch their dry tongues.
They sip and crunch,
hungry, thirsty, reminiscent -
the fire in their bellies still
rages on, full of
smokey vodka and a
vague, lingering embarrassment.

Oxford

My fingers burn incendiary
as they flicker down the denotive curve of your
body,
running from waist to hip and
back again.

Your hands play with fire as they
intertwine with my own in the
airless space between us -
we are tentative
at first,
cautious, but
the backdraft still doesn't scare us like it should.
In fact,
the backdraft doesn't scare us
at all.

Golden Hour

You wake like fire,
darling,
with the heat on your skin,
the sparks at your lips,
the ash in your mouth...
And, oh,
how you flicker,
sweet one,
incandescent one -
fragile one,
oh,
how you
flicker.

Molten

They call you
Volcano,
Danger,
Pompeii -
they tell me to
to evacuate,
to fly away
as if the floor were
Lava,
they swear that you'll
break me,
burn me,
drown me in
Magma and Ash.

I nod,
smile,
acquiesce;
I leave,
ignore,
return to Italy -
return
to you.

On Wintertime Hygge and Bittersweet Reminiscence

Your records are playing,
Grandma,
and the fireplace is alight
downstairs.
The scent of your candles
burns bright
in the air,
and I feel you beside me,
stroking my hair,
smiling.

We used to watch the fireworks together,
do you remember?
You always made us Parkin,
all ginger spice and crumbs on plates,
and we'd hide in the house,
too frightened of the noises to
leave.

You'd knit us scarves and
warm our hands between your own -
on days like today,
Grandma,
when all we have
left of you
are old records and candles,
I miss you more than ever.

Uprising

I rise from the ashes
like a
Phoenix ready to
Fight -
my breath hot,
my wings ablaze.

I am the Woman
of whom Men are
scared;
I will not bite my tongue,
I will not sit pretty and
I will *not* be afraid.

I will leap and I will spread,
determined, focused, incendiary -
I will scorch and leap and lick,
I will spark and flicker and fume,
I will burn in the name of
children, of generations yet to come,
I will transform into
the Phoenix, the Smoke, the Flame,
the Bonfire, the Stake, the Fuel:
do not underestimate me,
for am I more
than my appearance;
I am more than
ashes.

For Frieda and Nicholas

'Call Dr. Hoarder.'

Darlings,
there is no fire left in me -
no way to fight off the grey,
the burnt-out, the hollow.
I leave you with words and
little else;
I leave you with half-finished poems
and painstaking anthologies,
I leave you with paper, with ink,
with the fuel for a pyre,
yet I leave you with love,
with apologies,
with a father.
I leave you in flames,
yet I don't leave you
willingly.

35259122R00033

Printed in Poland
by Amazon Fulfillment
Poland Sp. z o.o., Wrocław